THE UPSIDE DOWN BUNNY

dào lì de tù zǐ
倒立的兔子

To our son Ethan,
May you always love who you are.

当朝阳悄悄从山顶探上来时，小兔子们开始一个个钻出洞来，来到绿油油软绵绵的草地上玩耍。

As the sun peeked over the hills of the green meadow, the bunnies began to play in the soft, green grass.

在这当中有一只与众不同的兔子，它的两颗门牙竟然
是长在下面的！

Among them, was one bunny who was a little different than
the others. His front teeth were upside down!

<ruby>这<rt>zhè</rt></ruby><ruby>一<rt>yī</rt></ruby><ruby>天<rt>tiān</rt></ruby>，<ruby>小<rt>xiǎo</rt></ruby><ruby>兔<rt>tù</rt></ruby><ruby>子<rt>zǐ</rt></ruby><ruby>正<rt>zhèng</rt></ruby><ruby>和<rt>hé</rt></ruby><ruby>朋<rt>péng</rt></ruby><ruby>友<rt>yǒu</rt></ruby><ruby>们<rt>men</rt></ruby><ruby>在<rt>zài</rt></ruby><ruby>草<rt>cǎo</rt></ruby><ruby>地<rt>dì</rt></ruby><ruby>上<rt>shàng</rt></ruby><ruby>玩<rt>wán</rt></ruby>。<ruby>突<rt>tū</rt></ruby><ruby>然<rt>rán</rt></ruby><ruby>间<rt>jiān</rt></ruby>，<ruby>它<rt>tā</rt></ruby><ruby>开<rt>kāi</rt></ruby><ruby>始<rt>shǐ</rt></ruby><ruby>特<rt>tè</rt></ruby><ruby>别<rt>bié</rt></ruby><ruby>在<rt>zài</rt></ruby><ruby>意<rt>yì</rt></ruby><ruby>自<rt>zì</rt></ruby><ruby>己<rt>jǐ</rt></ruby><ruby>的<rt>de</rt></ruby><ruby>牙<rt>yá</rt></ruby><ruby>齿<rt>chǐ</rt></ruby><ruby>和<rt>hé</rt></ruby><ruby>大<rt>dà</rt></ruby><ruby>家<rt>jiā</rt></ruby><ruby>不<rt>bù</rt></ruby><ruby>一<rt>yī</rt></ruby><ruby>样<rt>yàng</rt></ruby>。

That day, as he played with his friends in the meadow, he started to feel strange about his teeth being different.

两个朋友惊讶地说："啊，我们从来没有注意到呢！"接着它们飞奔到树后面，回来时拿了两大捆胡萝卜，问道："那你能吃胡萝卜吗？"

"Wow! We never noticed before!" his friends said surprised. They darted behind a tree and returned holding two bushels of carrots. "Can you eat carrots?" they asked.

小兔子们迅雷不及地吃完了一大堆胡萝卜。

The bunnies speedily munch through the giant pile of carrots with no problem.

"我吃得好撑！" 小兔子仰躺在地上说。

"你吃起胡萝卜来一点问题也没有呢！" 它的朋友们说，

"嘿！我们想到了一个好主意。"

"I am soooooo full!" said the bunny.

"It looks like you are great at eating carrots!" said his friends.

"Hey, we have an idea."

sān gè hǎo péng yǒu bèng bèng tiào tiào zhe lái dào le chí táng biān wàng zhe zì jǐ zài shuǐ lǐ
三个好朋友蹦蹦跳跳着来到了池塘边，望着自己在水里
de dǎo yǐng xiǎo tù zǐ shuō wā wǒ de yá chǐ zài shàng miàn le ne kě shì
的倒影。小兔子说："哇！我的牙齿在上面了呢，可是
nǐ liǎng de yá chǐ dǎo guò lái zài xià miàn le
你俩的牙齿倒过来在下面了。"

The three friends hopped over to the pond and looked into their
reflection. "Wow! My teeth are on top now, but now you two have
upside-down teeth," said the bunny.

两只小兔子互相看了看，惊讶道："真的，要不我们再试试别的方法？"

liǎng zhī xiǎo tù zǐ hù xiāng kàn le kàn， jīng yà dào： zhēn de， yào bù wǒ mén zài shì shì bié de fāng fǎ

The friends looked at each other with surprise. "You are right," they said. "Let's go try something else."

sān gè hǎo péng yǒu yòu bèng [tiào] [zhe] lái dào le fù jìn [de] shù lín lǐ tā mén měi rén [dōu] zhǎo
三个好朋友又蹦跳着来到了附近的树林里，他们每人都找

dào le yì zhǐ cū zhuàng jié shí de shù gān bǎ zì jǐ xuán guà le qǐ lái
到了一只粗壮结实的树干，把自己悬挂了起来。

The three friends hopped into the nearby woods and found a sturdy branch to dangle from.

小兔子说："太好玩啦！我的牙齿在上面了，可是你们的牙齿又倒过来了。"

"This is fun, but now my teeth are on top and yours are upside down again!" said the bunny.

突然，一个好主意闪现在小兔子的脑海中。

Suddenly, a wonderful idea popped into the bunny's mind.

xiǎo tù zǐ líng huó de yī gè gēn dòu [tóu] [cháo] xià dǎo lì le qǐ lái bìng huān hū dào
小兔子灵活地一个跟斗，头朝下倒立了起来并欢呼道，
tài hǎo lā zhè xià dà jiā de yá chǐ dōu zài shàng miàn lā
"太好啦！这下大家的牙齿都在上面啦！"

The bunny did a small tumble and stood on his head.
"Hooray! All of our teeth are on top now!"

sān gè hǎo péng yǒu yī zhì rèn wèi zhè gè zhǔ yì miào jí le　suǒ yǐ
三个好朋友一致认为这个主意妙极了，所以
tā men jiē xià lái yī zhěng tiān [dōu] shì [zhè] yàng wán [de]
它们接下来一整天都是这样玩的。

The friends thought this was very clever, so they
spent the rest of their day together like this.

它们去荡了秋千，又玩起了捉迷藏，直到金色的太阳开始慢慢地藏到绿油油的山坡后面。

They swung and played hide-and-seek until the sun started to set on the green meadow.

小兔子说：" 我玩累啦，
太阳也快下山了。我们该
回家啦！"

"I am tired and the sun is setting. I think it's time to head home," said the bunny.

xī yáng yuè lái yuè dī，sān gè hǎo péng
夕阳越来越低，三个好朋
yǒu yī gè jiē yī gè zài shān jiān de xiǎo
友一个接一个在山间的小
lù shàng cháo zhe jiā de fāng xiàng pǎo qù
路上朝着家的方向跑去。

As the sun sank lower and
lower, the three friends
scampered down the path to
their burrows.

到家门外时，三个好朋友停下拥抱再见。

"你倒立着，我们要怎么拥抱呢？"

"我也不知道，如果我转过来，
我的牙齿又会在下面了。"

At home, the three friends stopped for a goodbye hug.
"How will we hug you like this?" they asked.
"I don't know. If I turn over,
my teeth will be upside down," said the bunny.

"这不重要，"朋友们说。

"牙齿在上面的你是我们的朋友；

牙齿在下面的你也是我们的朋友；

我们喜欢无论什么样的你；

没有比和你在一起开心玩耍更重要的事。"

三个好朋友拥抱晚安，然后各自回到温暖的兔子窝。

"That doesn't matter," said the friends.
"You are our friend with right-side-up teeth.
You are our friend with upside-down teeth.
We like you just the way you are.
It's the fun we have together that matters."
They hugged and went into their warm burrows for the night.

xiǎo tù zi [hé] bà bà mā mā yì qǐ [zuān] jìn wēn nuǎn [de] [bèi] wō huí xiǎng [zhe] kuài [lè] [de] yì tiān
小兔子和爸爸妈妈一起钻进温暖的被窝，回想着快乐的一天，

mǎn liǎn guà [zhe] wēi xiào jìn rù [le] tián mì [de] mèng xiāng
满脸挂着微笑进入了甜蜜的梦乡。

The bunny snuggled into bed with his mommy and daddy, thinking of what great fun he had and fell asleep with a big smile.

^{wǎn} ^{ān} ^{xiǎo} ^{tù} ^{zǐ}
晚安，小兔子　Good Night, Bunny

^{wǎn} ^{ān} ^{mā} ^{mā}
晚安，妈妈　Good Night, Mama

^{wǎn} ^{ān} ^{bà} ^{bà}
晚安，爸爸　Good Night, Baba

^{wǎn} ^{ān} ^{péng} ^{yǒu} ^{mén}
晚安，朋友们　Good Night, Friends

^{wǎn} ^{ān} ^[dà] ^[jiā]
晚安，大家　Good Night, Everybody

wán

完

The End

This picture book was created and illustrated by Rui and written by Stephen, who became new parents in 2021. When their son Ethan had his first bottom teeth come in they joked that it made him look like an upside-down bunny, which inspired them to write this story.

Made in the USA
Middletown, DE
21 November 2022